Little Ant
and the Dragonfly

S.M.R. Saia

Illustrations by Tina Perko

Little Ant and the dragonfly were great friends, but they did not always see eye to eye. For example, Little Ant thought that living in a colony was the very best kind of life. The dragonfly, on the other hand, preferred to spend his days alone, in the air, and close to water.

Sometimes, when they were talking about their differences, Little Ant would go too far. "It's because ants are so smart that we are more successful than dragonflies," Little Ant told the dragonfly one day.

"More successful how?" the dragonfly asked.

"There are so many more of us," Little Ant said. "For every dragonfly you see, there must be hundreds — thousands — of ants."

The dragonfly was mild-mannered and kind, and he did not like to disagree with Little Ant, so he tended to keep his opinions to himself.

"Why do you let Little Ant walk all over you?" the other dragonflies sometimes asked him.

"I don't," the dragonfly would reply. "I don't mind a difference of opinion, and I don't think that most things are worth fighting about."

Even the other ants sometimes told the dragonfly, "Little Ant walks all over you." But the dragonfly didn't see it that way, and day after day, whenever he was out and about, and he spied Little Ant scurrying below him, he always took the time to swoop down and say hello.

One day, the dragonfly saw Little Ant near the edge of a puddle. He was with Buddy Ant, and they were trying to pull a rather large green pea out of the water.

The dragonfly made a lap around the puddle, watching his friends. He was about to land and ask if he could help, when a hummingbird suddenly shot past him and tumbled to the ground behind Little Ant and Buddy Ant.

Neither of the ants saw the hummingbird, but there was a tremor when she hit the ground. Buddy Ant lost his balance, pitched forward, and reached out his hand towards Little Ant to steady himself. Little Ant, still intent on his work, felt Buddy Ant shove him, hard, on the back before Little Ant tumbled headfirst into the water.

The startled hummingbird hopped up, fluttered her feathers, and zipped away before either of the ants could turn around. Little Ant stood up out of the puddle, sopping wet. He was furious. "I guess you think that's funny!" Little Ant said.

"I'm sorry," Buddy Ant said. "I lost my balance." The dragonfly landed beside them and quickly explained about the hummingbird.

"I didn't see a hummingbird," Little Ant insisted, "and I was standing right here."

"I didn't see a hummingbird either," Buddy Ant said, "but there could have been a hummingbird. Something made the ground tremble. Something made me feel like I was going to fall."

"Little Ant, I saw the hummingbird," the dragonfly explained. "Buddy Ant didn't mean to push you."

"So you saw Buddy Ant push me!" Little Ant exclaimed. "You can be my witness."

"I am happy to tell the others what I saw," the dragonfly said. Little Ant was pleased. Since the dragonfly seldom argued with Little Ant, Little Ant was sure that the dragonfly would tell the others Little Ant's side of the story.

All evening, Little Ant told anyone who would listen that Buddy Ant had attacked him at the puddle's edge. By the next morning, when it came time to present his case against Buddy Ant, there had been so much gossip about the incident that a crowd of insects of all types had gathered around to see what would happen.

Little Ant stood smug and confident in front of the crowd and told his side of the story. When he was finished, he called the dragonfly to be his witness.

"Tell everyone what you saw," Little Ant said. So the dragonfly told all the insects about the clumsy hummingbird. Everyone gasped.

"That is not what happened!" Little Ant declared. But by the time that Buddy Ant finished telling his side of the story, all the other insects believed in the hummingbird, too.

"I am sorry, Little Ant," the dragonfly said when it was all over. "You asked me to tell them what I saw, and I told the truth."

"You are obviously not my friend either," Little Ant said, and he turned and walked away.

Uncle Ant, who was standing nearby, called after him: "Little Ant, I wish you would reconsider!" But Little Ant didn't stop. He knew what he had seen, and he knew what had happened, and as far as he was concerned, any insect who thought differently was just plain wrong.

All of the other ants thought that Little Ant was being unreasonable, and this made Little Ant even angrier. He avoided the other ants, and began to stay away from the anthill until very late in the day. One evening, as he was coming home, a shadow swooped across Little Ant and frightened him. There was a flutter and a thud, and a hummingbird flew directly into the anthill, knocking part of it over. The hummingbird quickly recovered and flew away again, and by the time the startled ants started pouring out of the anthill, the hummingbird was gone.

The ants were angry. They knew Little Ant had a bad attitude, and they thought that he had destroyed the anthill on purpose. "I didn't do this!" Little Ant said. "A hummingbird flew into the anthill, knocked it over, and then flew away!"

"We did not see a hummingbird," the other ants said. "All we see here is you."

"I was wrong before," Little Ant tried to convince them. "There is a clumsy hummingbird!"

Little Ant insisted that he was innocent, but no one believed him. Little Ant felt close to tears. He had behaved badly, and now he didn't have a single friend in all of the anthill. Just then the dragonfly, who had been hovering overhead and listening to the conversation, landed nearby.

"I believe you, Little Ant," the dragonfly said.

Uncle Ant stepped forward and said, "So do I."

"Buddy Ant, I am sorry I said that you shoved me into the puddle on purpose," Little Ant said. "I believe there was a hummingbird. I believe it was an accident. I should have believed you, even though I didn't see the hummingbird myself, because we are friends."

"Every truth has two sides," Uncle Ant told all the ants. "Just because someone sees things differently than you do, doesn't mean they're wrong."

After that, whenever the dragonfly told Little Ant things that he couldn't even imagine, rather than argue with him, Little Ant would listen, and marvel that he lived in a world where maybe, just possibly, such a thing could be true.

Published by Shelf Space Books
ISBN: 978-1-945713-22-4

CPSIA information can be obtained
at www.ICGtesting.com
Printed in the USA
JSHW030720250421
13921JS00002B/28